This Book Belongs to

..................................................................................

..................................................................................

D0177105

90710 000 410 559

For Sohana
My beautiful clever daughter, who smiles through her pain
but never stops hoping to fly in the future – S.C.

London Borough of Richmond Upon Thames

RTK

90710 000 410 559

Askews & Holts

JF    £6.99

9781910959688

Text copyright © Sharmila Collins 2019
Illustrations copyright © Carolina Rabei 2019

The right of Sharmila Collins and Carolina Rabei to be identified as the author and illustrator of this work has been asserted by them in accordance with the Copyright, Designs and Patents Act, 1988 (United Kingdom).

First published in Great Britain and in the USA in 2019 by
Otter-Barry Books
Little Orchard, Burley Gate, Hereford, HR1 3QS
www.otterbarrybooks.com

All rights reserved

No part of this publication may be reproduced, stored in a retrieval system, or transmitted, in any form, or by any means, electrical, mechanical, photocopying, recording or otherwise without the prior written permission of the publisher or a licence permitting restricted copying. In the United Kingdom such licences are issued by the Copyright Licensing Agency, Barnards Inn, 86 Fetter Lane, London EC4A1EN.

A catalogue record for this book is available from the British Library.

Designed by Arianna Osti

ISBN 978-1-91095-968-8

Illustrations created digitally

Printed in China

1 3 5 7 9 8 6 4 2

# Binky's Time to Fly!

SHARMILA COLLINS

Illustrated by
CAROLINA RABEI

Otter-Barry BOOKS

Binky was waiting.

First he was an egg.

Then he was a hungry caterpillar.

Now he was in a cocoon.

But what he really wanted to be was a **butterfly**, with big and beautiful wings.

At last the day came!

The sun was shining and its warmth
gave Binky strength.

He pushed and pushed...

and cracked his cocoon...
and...

out he came to say

'Hello' to the world.

BUT

when Binky opened his wings

they didn't work.

They were weak and pale, silvery, wispy and unfinished.

They had a wing shape and a wing frame

but only a few strands

and holes instead of colour.

And they would not and could not let him fly.

Binky hung his head low.

His heart was full of sorrow

and disappointed dreams.

His fragile wings shimmered

in the pale moonlight.

What could he do?

He slunk away and hid under a leaf,

unhappy at being different,

too shocked and scared to find help.

Two crows came along to see if Binky was worth eating,
but they stared and laughed at him instead.

"There isn't much to eat on *him*," they cawed,
and flew away.

But then two butterflies, who had been caterpillars
at the same time as Binky, came to find him.

"We will help you," they said.

"Together we can fix your wings."

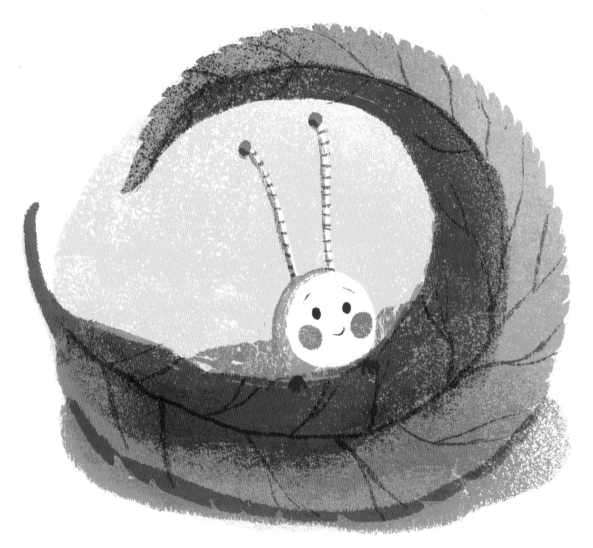

Binky crept out from behind his leaf and smiled.

Might he be able to fly after all?

First the butterflies found a friendly blue-tit
to carry Binky to the zoo.

There they found silkworms
munching on mulberry leaves

and spiders busily
making their webs.

"Please, will you help us mend Binky's wings?"
the butterflies asked.

The silkworms and spiders were glad to help.
The silkworms spun fine silver silk thread
and the spiders wove the threads into Binky's wings,
to make them strong.
Then they asked the bees to inject them with all
the colours of the rainbow,
in wild and intricate patterns.

Binky stayed very still and the butterflies fluttered above,
until at last the work was finished.
The silkworms, spiders and bees stood back,
admiring their handiwork.
"It's amazing what we can do if we all work together!"
they said to each other.

But Binky still had his eyes shut!

"Open up your **wings**, Binky,"

they all called together.

Binky took a deep breath. Very, very slowly, he opened up his wings.

His heart was full of hope and longing.

Were the wings strong?

Would they lift him into the air? Would they let him fly?

His wings felt heavier and more robust,

they felt as if they might let him fly.

Binky opened his eyes...

The wings were magnificent!
They were strong!
There were no holes... just woven silk threads
with bold and beautiful colours.

"I am different to all other butterflies, and I always will be," said Binky. "But I don't care – all I want to do is fly."

Thank you!

He thanked all his new friends, the butterflies, the blue-tit, the silkworms, the spiders and the bees.

The butterflies rose into the air
and fluttered above him.
"Come on, Binky," they called.

"It's time to fly!"

Binky tested his wings, opening them carefully,

once, twice, three times... and then...

carefree and happy, the silver in his wings glinting in the sun,

Binky rose up into the air

and FLEW

to join his friends!

# Note from the Author

This is a book about hope – and the flying is about freedom.

EB (epidermolysis bullosa) is a fragile skin condition that causes blistering, skin loss and malignant skin cancer in severe types. There is no cure as yet, and 500,000 people worldwide live with it. Children with EB are said to have 'skin as fragile as a butterfly's wings' and are often called 'butterfly children'. Their skin is fragile but they are not.

These children live a very painful life with strength, humour and spirit. They have wounds dressed and blisters pricked every day. They experience difficulty eating because of mouth and throat blisters, difficulty walking because of blistering on their legs and feet and sometimes they cannot see because of blisters on their eye surfaces. Even a small bump or rub can cause a tear or blister, excluding them from rough games and sport. They rise to the challenge of life every day, including stares and on occasions mockery, and live with the hope that one day they will be free from pain.

My daughter, Sohana, has severe recessive dystrophic epidermolysis bullosa. Her positive spirit and resilience, despite her life's challenges, fill me with admiration. Watching and participating in her pain inspired the foundation of a charity, Cure EB, www.cure-eb.org, which funds research and clinical trials towards effective treatments and eventually a cure.

Sohana named a butterfly 'Binky' for one of our campaigns and I wrote this story around that name.

Sharmila Collins
*Founder, Cure EB*

All author royalties go to www.cure-eb.org

# About the Author
# and Illustrator

Sharmila Collins was born in Sri Lanka but has lived in the UK
for more than 40 years. She qualified from Cambridge University with
an MA VetMB MRCVS and worked as a veterinary surgeon until soon after
her first child, Sohana, was born. Jacinda and the twins, Akhaila and Zuleikha,
followed in fairly quick succession. In 2011, she founded the charity Cure EB
with husband James to accelerate research into treatments for epidermolysis
bullosa. Her dearest wish is to see this intensely cruel condition treated.
She lives in Islington, North London, and also has a little dog called Fizzle.
*Binky's Time to Fly* is her first book.

· · ·

Ever since she was very small, Carolina Rabei loved drawing.
She has dedicated eight years of her life to the study of Fine Art, attaining a
BA in Graphic Design in Moldova and then achieving a distinction in Children's
Book Illustration at the prestigious Cambridge School of Art in 2014.
Carolina's debut picture book, *Snow*, illustrating Walter de la Mare's poem,
was published to critical acclaim: it was nominated for the esteemed Kate
Greenaway Medal. Carolina went on to illustrate more of Walter de la Mare's
work: *The Ride-by-Nights, Summer Evening* and *Silver*. She also writes her own
stories. One of them is *Crunch!*, which was shortlisted for the Read It Again!
competition in 2016 and has been translated into five languages.
Carolina loves working on a diverse range of projects and her artwork
reveals a unique mix of traditional as well as digital techniques.